F R A S E R

Maggie

ADVENTURES OF
FRASER
THE YELLOW DOG

RESCUE ON ASPEN MOUNTAIN

BY JILL SHEELEY

ILLUSTRATED BY TAMMIE LANE

COURTNEY PRESS

First edition published in 2002 by Courtney Press, Aspen, Colorado
Copyright © 2002 by Jill Sheeley

A very special thanks to Rob Seideman, Tammie Lane, my family and all my many friends who gave me advice and support.

Thanks to Missen Brucker whose chocolate chip cookie recipe was chosen above all the others for the yummiest melt-in-your-mouth chocolate chip cookie. It won the hearts and tummies of the Aspen Girl Scout Troop #257, who were kind enough to test the final six cookies!

Aspen Skiing Company's logo used with permission. Aspen Skiing Company, L.L.C.

Library of Congress Control Number: 2001097725

For information about ordering this book, write: Jill Sheeley • P.O. Box 845 • Aspen, CO 81612 or email aac@rof.net. Check out our website: JillSheeleybooks.com

Printed in Korea.
ISBN 0-9609108 7-5

This book is dedicated to Rochelle Broughton, a wonderful 11-year old girl who lives in Aspen. Rochelle is physically challenged. She has endured numerous operations with strength and courage, and yet always has a smile on her face. She has a "can do" attitude and is respected by her peers. Rochelle is an inspiration to us all.

Partial proceeds from this book will benefit Andrea Jaeger's Silver Lining Ranch in Aspen–a magical world created for children with cancer.

The 11-bedroom Aspen ranch is located on a gentle stream with beautiful views of the surrounding mountains. This ranch provides a chance for children with cancer to be free to be kids — to laugh and enjoy all the activities of the Rocky Mountains.

Andrea's vision involves engaging children in inspirational opportunities that develop hope and courage in order to battle their illnesses.

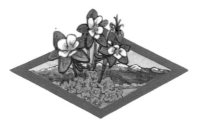

ey, Fraser," said Courtney, "aren't you excited about our big hike today?"

Fraser barked three times, then took off running.

"Fraser, where are you running now? You've been chasing tennis balls all morning. Soon, you'll be running laps around us."

Courtney looked up and saw Fraser greeting Katy and Taylor.

"Sorry we're late, Courtney, but it took us forever to pack the picnic lunch. We even brought a special treat for Fraser— a nutritious PowerBone®," said Taylor.

"Thanks guys," said Courtney. "And I brought first aid gear, my dad's climbing rope, and our radio phone. You just never know!"

"Fraser looks ready," said Katy. "Let's go."

The girls hoisted their packs onto their backs and began hiking up Aspen Mountain.

They had been hiking all summer. They were preparing for their school backpacking trip. Courtney knew it would be much easier if they got used to carrying a heavy pack. She also wanted to make sure that their hiking boots were comfortable.

The girls planned to hike to the top of the mountain, walk along the ridge, do a loop, and end up back at the gondola for the ride down.

"It sure feels steeper hiking up Little Nell than it does skiing down," said Courtney.

"We sure know how to pick the day," exclaimed Taylor. "It is so beautiful. Can you believe how blue the sky is?"

"Wow," said Katy, "look at these wildflowers." The sweet scent caught her nose.

"The colors are so bright," added Taylor. "It looks like a painting."

"Did you know that the word 'daisy' means *day's eye?*" asked Katy. "European settlers brought daisy seeds to America years ago."

"Indian Paintbrush are my favorite flowers," said Courtney. "I love the old Indian legend of the boy painting rainbows in the sky."

"Yowee," said Taylor, "I have never seen so many Columbines. Did you know that the Blue Columbine is the Colorado state flower?"

"This has been the best summer for wildflowers," said Courtney.

"I agree," said Katy. "This has been the most awesome summer. Think of all the fun we had..."

Horseback riding...

Kayaking...

Soccer...

"Wow," said Courtney, "we're already at the top. Look at these amazing views."

"I can see Aspen Highlands," said Katy.

"And there's Mount Hayden," chimed in Taylor.

"Let's stop and have our picnic on the ridge," said Courtney. "We shouldn't waste too much time, though. We still have a long way to go if we want to hike the loop."

The girls were warm and happy, having conquered the hardest part of the hike.

"Yum," said Katy, "peanut butter, honey and banana sandwiches are my favorite."

"I know that it's really important to drink lots of water," said Taylor, "but I sure am glad you brought your melt-in-your-mouth chocolate chip cookies, Courtney!"

Suddenly, Fraser, who had been quietly resting and eating his dog bone, took off running at lightning speed.

The girls followed Fraser, running as fast as their legs would take them.

Fraser came to a sudden stop. His tail was frantically wagging, and he was barking as loudly as Courtney had ever heard him.

"What's wrong, boy?" asked Katy.

As soon as the girls got to the spot where Fraser was standing, they knew.

The mine shaft was 15-20 feet deep. From way down below, they could barely hear the faint whimpering of a dog. As they looked down the dark hole, they could see a figure with bright eyes peering up at them. This pup was in big trouble.

Courtney, Taylor and Katy stared down inside the hole.

"What are we going to do?" asked Taylor.

"I have no idea," said Katy.

Courtney looked at Fraser who was pulling a rope out of her pack. "I think Fraser has a plan to rescue this poor pup!" exclaimed Courtney. "Let's help."

Taylor scrambled through her backpack and found her flashlight.

"See, Courtney," said Taylor, "it's a good thing you remembered to bring your dad's climbing rope."

"I think I know exactly what Fraser has up his sleeve," said Courtney.

"I trust Fraser," said Taylor. "He's never failed us yet."

"You can say that again!" agreed Katy.

Courtney quickly took everything out of her pack, and placed two of Fraser's favorite dog bones inside. They tied a rope to the pack, and lowered it down the deep, dark mine shaft.

"I sure hope this works," said Courtney anxiously. "I hope that pup is so hungry it jumps right in and gobbles down those yummy treats."

"Okay, Fraser," yelled Courtney, "the pup took the bait and is in the pack. Pull, Fraser, pull as hard as you can!"

"What do you think happened?" asked Katy.

"I'm not sure,"said Courtney. "She must be lost."

"Oh my gosh," cried Taylor, "I've almost got the pack!"

"Here, little pup," said Courtney, "drink this water. You must be as thirsty as a camel."

"Now what?"asked Katy.

"I'll use the radio phone to call our vet," said Courtney. "Maybe Rosemary can meet us by the gondola."

"We can build a *travois* (trav•wah)," offered Taylor, "just like we did in our winter survival class."

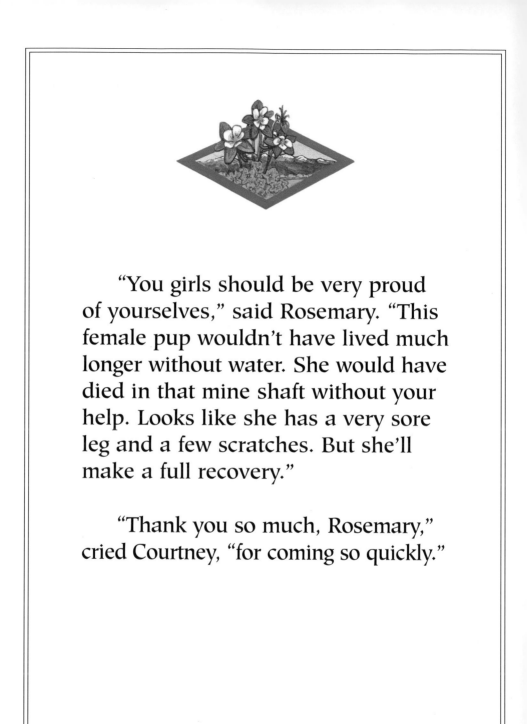

"You girls should be very proud of yourselves," said Rosemary. "This female pup wouldn't have lived much longer without water. She would have died in that mine shaft without your help. Looks like she has a very sore leg and a few scratches. But she'll make a full recovery."

"Thank you so much, Rosemary," cried Courtney, "for coming so quickly."

Courtney looked at Fraser. He was a real hero.

"Look, girls," exclaimed Rosemary, "there's a note on the pup's collar."

The girls bent down and Courtney read the note. "Hi, my name is Maggie. I am a little puppy. I regret to say that my owner had to leave town and couldn't take me. If you find me, please adopt me and give me a good home. I'm very sweet and well-behaved."

"Wow," said Taylor looking at Courtney, "I think that you and Fraser have a new member of the family!"

Maggie lifted her head and licked Fraser's face.

"Just think, Fraser," said Courtney, "we can take Maggie on our next adventure!"

Courtney's Melt-in-your-mouth · Chocolate Chip Cookies ·

Preheat oven to 375°

INGREDIENTS

1 C (2 sticks) butter
½ C granulated sugar
¾ C brown sugar
1 large egg
2 t vanilla

¾ t baking powder
¼ t salt
2¼ C flour
2 c your favorite
     chocolate chips

Cream together the butter, sugars & the egg. Blend in vanilla, baking powder & salt. Then add the flour. Finally add the chocolate chips & mix well. Bake for 12-15 minutes.

Two tricks: use an ice cream scooper to scoop the batter onto a cookie sheet lined with parchment paper. Only cook one cookie sheet at a time — the cookies bake more evenly. Cool on a wire rack. While they're still warm, they'll definitely melt in your mouth!! Enjoy.